Welcome to The Giggle Club

The Giggle Club is a collection of picture books made to put a giggle into early reading. There are funny stories about a contrary mouse, a dancing fox, a turtle with a trumpet, a pig with a ball, a hungry monster, a wide-mouthed frog, an elephant who sneezes away the jungle and lots more! Each of these characters is a member of **The Giggle Club**, but anyone can join: just pick up a **Giggle Club** book, read it and get giggling!

Turn to the checklist on the inside back cover and check off the Giggle Club books you have read.

For Jack
D. D.

For Mum, Dad, Jess and Ella
T. F.

PET WASH
written by
Dayle Ann Dodds
illustrated by Tor Freeman
WALKER BOOKS
AND SUBSIDIARIES
LONDON • BOSTON • SYDNEY

STEP RIGHT UP!
Get in line.
We'll wash your pets
and make them shine.

We'll rub. We'll scrub.
We're
WALLY and GENE.

There's not a pet
that we can't clean.

WASH YOUR CAT?

We can do that!
Spick and span in no time flat.

WASH YOUR BEAR?

With loving care.

We'll even style and curl his hair.

WASH YOUR EEL?

It's no big deal.

We'll dry him on our eel-mobile.

WASH
YOUR RACCOON?
He'll shine like the
moon.

YOUR KANGAROO?

With mint shampoo.

CROCODILE?
With a
smile.

A TINY ANT?
Who says
we
can't?

SEAL?
Deal.

RHINO?
Fine-O.

HIPPO?
Zippo!

Big or small or
in-between,
nothing's
too hard
for
WALLY
and
GENE.

Excuse me!
Can you wash my ...

baby brother?

SORRY!
PET

WE'RE CLOSED!

First published 2001 by Walker Books Ltd
87 Vauxhall Walk, London SE11 5HJ

10 9 8 7 6 5 4 3 2 1

This book has been typeset in 'ela' Tapioca.
The pictures were done in acrylic.

Printed in Hong Kong

British Library Cataloguing in Publication Data
A catalogue record for this book is available
from the British Library.

ISBN 0-7445-7392-0 (hb)
ISBN 0-7445-7393-9 (pb)

Giggle Club Jokes!
Why do giraffes have such long necks?
They can't stand the smell of their feet!